Siggi Selector

Flying from flower to flower

Imprint:

Titel:

The Beauty was the Beast

Erotic Pick Up Adventure with Bad Ending

Author:

Siggi Selector © 2018

Coverphoto © (c) Alexvolot | Dreamstime.com

The photo was edited Siggi Selector

Bibliografische Information der Deutschen Nationalbibliothek:
Die Deutsche Nationalbibliothek verzeichnet diese Publikation
in der Deutschen Nationalbibliografie; detaillierte bibliografische Daten sind im Internet über http://dnb.d-nb.de abrufbar.

Printing and Publishing:

Books on Demand GmbH, Norderstedt

ISBN: 9783748168874

Content

The Beauty was the Beast

Erotic Pick Up Adventure with Bad Ending..

Disclaimer:

Do not read the story if you mind explicit language.

The landing is followed by the departure

The Pick Up Game

Isabel was a dream woman in her mid-twenties and had made the mistake of standing alone at the bar in the café-bistro room of the big disco-club. At a time when hardly anyone went out and therefore only a few people were in the club. So she had absolutely no competition compared to the few female guests already present. She was definitely the prettiest girl in the big, not yet crowded club.

I was her age and I knew all the flirting tricks of a pick-up-artist. Moreover, I looked pretty good at the time. I had full, dark hair, a good figure, a job in the advertising industry and a car.

Because I never fell in love when I saw a pretty girl, I could confidently approach her. Quickly the girls became interested in me, the cool guy, and I seduced them.

When I saw Isabel, the most beautiful of all the beauties, I knew that flirting would be difficult.

But I would not care about a failure either. So I started the approach, sat next to her. She certainly expected a stupid pickup line of one of this kind:

Hello, who are you, what's your name, what are you doing so early in the club, where are you from, are you here more often and let's dance together or drink together?

Pickup lines like these only work among teenagers without experience, but certainly not with this woman.

This woman was no longer an unexperienced girl. She was in her mid-twenties. She had long, black hair that was interestingly hair dressed and into which she had dyed a silver stripe. Her top figure was wrapped in a sexy tailored summer dress that showed a bit of her medium-sized breast, which she was surely proud of, otherwise she would not wear exactly this dress. In addition, it was super fitting to her body and was slotted, so you could see her beautiful legs that ended in high heels shoes.

All in all, you could see that she had the money for such a great outfit.

Her skin was tanned as if she just had been on a vacation somewhere with a beach. Surely she was one hundred percent aware of her charisma

She had heard these stupid starters of unimaginative men often enough, and they for sure gave her a pain in the ass and all these green bunglers bored her.

Well, she was here in this disco club. Why do girls go alone to a club? Ha, ha, they are hoping to finally get to know an interesting guy.

To be successful I had to do something different, had to say something that she never ever had heard as a starter.

I sat next to her, without looking at her and without saying a word to her. I ordered a mineral water from the bartender.

Then I looked around to see what was happening around me and, surprise, I found that she was sitting coincidentally next to me.

I looked into her face without saying anything.

She said: "No."

Just like that.

She said the answer "no" even before I even asked her any question.

With that she confirmed my prejudice about her

"I did not want to ask that," I said.

"So? Well what did you want to say?" she asked snippily.

"I wanted to ask you: Hey, what do you do tomorrow afternoon," I said cool, looking straight into her eyes.

"That's none of your business!", she said curtly, trying to avoid my gaze.

"I understand," I said. "I do not want to ask you further what you intend to do tomorrow afternoon, but no matter what you intend to do, I have a better suggestion: It's such a beautiful summer weather and you and me, we can meet and have an ice cream together or we go sunbathing at a lake or we do both: Let's eat ice-cream at the lake."

"Aha. Anything better didn't come to your mind?" She provoked me.

"Well, it would at least be good enough to get to know each other better. But as I guess, maybe you do not want to date a stranger who you don't know."

"That's exactly how it is," she said.

Without saying anything, I took my glass, got up from the bar stool, left her, and walked a few steps into the room. But only to turn around again and come back to her.

I put the drink back in place but I did not sit down again. Instead, I reached out my hand to greet and shake hands, saying:

"Hello, may I introduce myself, my name is Siggi and I would like to know you. May I sit next to you?"

She had already thought that she had won again and the guy (me) had given up and had walked away. Now she was so surprised by my second flirt-attack that she should have laughed about it.

But she controlled herself, and I could only make out the brief start of a slight smile around the corner of her mouth. The same moment she had her "leave me alone" expression in her face again and said: "And what if I DO NOT want to know you?"

"Then you have no chance of eating ice cream at the lake with me, because you do not want to make an appointment with strangers."

Now she could not help laughing. But just like a lady she only smiled briefly and pretended as if she had already known the joke.

"Do you always approach women like that?" she asked me.

Her body language signaled to me that now she was much more willing to engage in a conversation with me. Besides, she had actually asked me something to answer and had not said something that was dismissive like everything else she had said before.

"No, I do not usually approach women like that, but if you want, I'll do it the way you already know and are used to. Maybe I'll have more chances to get to know you then?"

"Well, then give it another try. Now I'm curious."

"Okay. I have to leave you now again. Stay seated! Do not run away, I'll be right back."

She nodded expectantly, and she was clearly enjoying joining in this pickup game.

Why not? It was exciting, also for her.

Again I turned around, left her, and took a few steps away. Turned around, came back to her.

Then I hunched, anxiously tucking my head in and stammering the following words like a shy boy, using a dialect she should know:

"Uh, sorry. You are all alone here. I just wanted to ask if you would like to dance with me? Maybe? Please?"

That made her day. I had won: She burst into a laughing out loud and even spanked her thighs. I joined her laughter and we laughed together like we had not laughed that good for a long time and we could not stop laughing and she was sitting on the bar stool, her body shaking with laughter and I was standing in front of her and tried not to roll on the floor laughing.

Then, without her permission, I sat down on the bar stool next to her again and watched her slowly calm down from laughing.

Then I asked, "Are you going to say NO again?"

"Which question?" She asked me.

"You should know it. You started to say "NO" to questions which I have not asked yet."

"You're really good," she said and immediately she regretted what she had said and stopped talking.

"Okay. So we will have some ice cream together, tomorrow afternoon? "

"No, I do not know you yet and I do not meet with men I do not know."

"Are you again starting to turn me down?"

"No. Now I want to get to know you. Come on, let's go dancing," she said, getting up and handing me a bill and a key.

"What's this?"

"My money and my key. I do not have a pocket in my dress and I do not have a handbag with me either. Please take care of it, keep it in your jeans pocket while we dance."

I was amazed and stared at the red dress on her beautiful body. Indeed. It nestled close to her dream figure and had no pockets. Also there was no handbag in sight. She had entrusted me all her cash and asked me to dance with her. Wow.

On the dance floor, she beamed at me like a nondescript girl who was happy that a boy had finally asked her to dance. And now I danced with this lady in red, who was happy that she had finally been addressed not by a beginner, but by a brave, imaginative man.

I knew that this flirtation would not end with a quick blowjob on the loo, but better.

That same evening, she did not go to bed with me, but we exchanged the phone numbers.

Roll Play Game at the Lake

The next day I called her and we arranged for a meeting at the lake, near the cafe on the beach.

When I got there and looked around a little, I saw that she was already there.

Isabel lay face down on her bath towel and was engrossed in reading a book.

Illustration:

This photo is NOT showing Isabel yet another pretty model, lying topless at the beach, reading a magazine. Isabel of my story was NOT topless.

I also lay on my stomach, right in front of her. She noticed it, looked up from the book for a moment.

Even before she could say something, I asked her:

"Please read me from your book."

She laughed and said, "No. Why should I?"

"So I know what you are reading and maybe we can talk about it."

"I read a vampire novel."

"Wow. One of those where the vampires are evil and are killed with wooden sticks through the heart, or one of the kind where the vampire falls in love with a beautiful girl like you and spares her?"

"A love novel with vampires of course."

"Typical woman," I blasphemed, "you misjudge the reality. Vampires are dead, they cannot feel anything."

"The one in this book, that's just a half-vampire."

"If he bites her, does she become a half-vampire?"

"I have not read so far. He has not bitten her yet."

"Imagine, Isabel, I would be a vampire, too. Imagine you are not lying on the bath towel but on your bed. "

I got up, took a few steps back, and spread my arms like an eagle's wings.

"You left the bedroom window open and I fly in to your room and land on you, on your back and take possession of you."

I spoke it and did it. Now I lay beside her, very close to her, one arm across her back and whispered in her ear:

"Now I bite you and suck your innocent blood into me."

I nibbled something on her neck and muttered:

"But I'm a real vampire, not half. I have no feelings, but you're mine forever, for the next million years, no, for all eternity. "

Then I kissed her wetly on the neck, without making a hickey. Isabel turned on her back, looked up at me and breathed:

"Now I'm yours, you vampire, and I'll prove to you that you have feelings as well, for you've just kissed Sleeping Beauty out of the magical sleep, and she also has magic and can finish your vampire life so you can become human again."

She spoke it and kissed my mouth. It evolved into a passionate kissing and, as I lay so close to her body, she felt my feelings solidify in my bathing trunks.

To be sure, she put her hand between my legs, briefly interrupted the kiss and mumbled, still close to my mouth:

"You cannot fool me, you are no longer a vampire, I have enchanted you and breathed life back into you and now you have feelings again."

At the word feelings, she grabbed my cock with her hand as tight as she could. I already had a strong boner under the thin fabric of the swimming trunks. She felt it. And she squeezed it.

"Ahh," I moaned and I slipped on my stomach, so not all people at the lake could see how horny I was.

"Ha, ha," she laughed, "I think we need to get into the water now so that your so-called feelings get some kind of cold shower. Come on, come on!"

We jumped up and laughing, we ran into the water until it reached to our chest. Then we fell around our necks and kissed each other. Under the surface of the water we fingered each other's crotchal area, so that there was no chance of cooling down in the water.

She took my cock out of the trunks and began to jerk vigorously, and entering from the side of the swimsuit, I drilled my finger into her pussy.

I was so horny and I whispered while kissing:

"Please do not stop, your vampire has never been so hot in cold water."

So she kept jerking and let me caress her pussy. As if my cock would be a leash, she pulled me deeper into the water, farther away from other bathers and she kneaded and squeezed and jerked my cock until my orgasm overwhelmed me. My legs buckled and I almost drowned.

Shuddering, I came back up, spitting water out of my mouth. She laughed loudly and I happily stared at her. I kissed her mouth again and grabbed her again in the crotch. But she fended me off, stopped kissing and said:

"No, not here, my ex-vampire. Let's go to my house, I'd rather get down in bed than in the water. "

In Bed with Isabel

She drove with her car, and I drove with mine, following her to her apartment. She lived on the third floor of a tenement. She walked up the stairs in front of me. All the way up, I saw her beautiful legs under the miniskirt, which barely covered her ass. I was looking forward to the next sex adventure with Isabel. The quick pick up success I had thanks to my vampire RPG story, which came to my mind spontaneously just because she happened read a vampire book.

It was quite easy for me to play this role-playing game convincingly, because vampires have no emotions and no feelings of love. As I don't.

Softies turn into machos through the loss of love, but women cannot turn machos into softies again, just with either kisses or sex.

Isabel did not know that. She had said "I have enchanted you", but that was not true. She had just made me horny.

Once in the apartment, Isabel showed me the kitchen, bathroom, bedroom, then, in the living room, she turned on music and disappeared into the bathroom, leaving me alone in the living room.

From the bathroom, she laughingly shouted:

"You can go to bed, I'll be right with you!"

Because I'm used to it, I first unpacked my trouser pockets. I put car keys, purse, chewing gum, lighter, and cigarettes on the table next to her handbag. Then I took off my shoes. Because it was summer, I did not wear socks. I put my shirt, trousers and underpants on an armchair and went naked into her bedroom. I pulled the blanket off the bed, folded it and put it on a chair. Then I lay back on the sheet and waited for Isabel. I was naked, as nature had made me.

It was not long before she came to my bedroom. She was just wrapped in a big, white bath towel,

But instead of opening the bath towel slowly and in slow motion so that I would have a nice treat for my eyes and a visual foreplay, she rushed at me, threw her body on mine, still holding the towel.

Isabel kissed me stormy and grabbed me wildly and wildly on the balls and tube and jerked my cock up. I got horny again, although the bath towel between her and me disturbed me, because I did not even feel her bare skin on mine.

As soon as Isabel realized that my cock had the necessary strength for the penetration into her pussy, she slid down from me, went to all fours in the doggy position and groaned: "Take me from behind!"

Okay, her wish was my command and I took her from behind. It bothered me a bit that I still had not yet seen her bare bosom, which had been so beautiful under her summer dress and the bikini swimsuit, I'm a tit fetishist!

I changed the position by pushing her out of the Doggystyle position and forced her on her back, into the missionary position.

But as soon as she lay under me, I again had no way to see her breasts, because she immediately hugged my neck and pulled my head down to her. My head was beside her, next to her neck and she clung tightly to me as if she kept me in a police grip.

I wanted to push me up with my arms to gain distance, but she clung so hard that I could not free myself.

At the same time, she clung her legs around my hips and hooked them over my butt so that I could not move freely in and out, but I was pressed tightly against her abdomen by her legs. I had no chance to set the rhythm or take her to any other position She just did not allow it.

I moaned, "Ride me!"

But Isabel did not respond, but groaned and shouted: "Yes, go on!"

I said, "Yes, I go on, but get up! Ride me!"

"No, I can only come to orgasm when the man is above me, in this position. Go on, fuck me, yes, go on, yes! Just like that!"

So I did not get out of this missionary position and only saw her face, but not her body. She simply did not allow it. Because of her tight grasp I could not switch to a more comfortable push-up, where I could see from some distance her whole body in which I penetrated.

"Show me your feelings, vampire, cum in me!", she commanded me and I hammered my cock into her harder and faster and penetrated deeper.

Isabel groaned loudly and shouted words like: "Deeper, yes, harder, ah, faster, ah," and I knew immediately that her moaning like in a porn film was acted. Then she got an orgasm.

She screamed, "I'm coming! I'm coming!"

Her climax was a great performance show. But I was not deceived and did not allow her any rest and although her fake groaning subsided, I still penetrated hard and persistently into her, as she had demanded before, when she had screamed: Deeper, harder, faster.

Now she asked me to come: "Yes, come on, my vampire, cum in me, yes, cum, cum, give it to me, cum, yes, cum, cum!" All that porn sound.

I had a slight feeling that this acting-show of her and the forced position in which I stuck was not good for my erection. So I looked into her beautiful face, imagining she was standing in front of me in the summer dress at the bar in the disco-club where we met. And I fucked her with her red dress on. This picture in my head helped my cock to stay strong.

I continued hammering and shouted:

"No, first you must come!"

And as soon as I had said it, she performed her second orgasm: "Yes, yes, that's good, oh, ohhh, yeah, I'm cuming, I'm cuming , ahhh! Ahh, ahh!"

I imagined she would have her orgasm in the dress and although the orgasm was played, my imagination managed to deceive myself. I looked into her beautiful face, on her mouth moaning those yes and ahh sounds and I felt how my orgasm was about to approach.

Suddenly I remembered that I was trapped between her long legs and if I did not manage to get out of that jail, I would orgasm into her. But I did not want to impregnate her. I did not know if she took the pill for birth control.

I was just before my cumshot and now fought my way out of their grip with all my strength and power. I pulled my cock out of her pussy, tore away her bath towel off the body, grabbed my penis and jerked myself during the ejaculations and my sperm flew over the naked body lying in front of me. My juices rained on her wrinkled stomach and splashed up to her breasts, which were large but limp and slid to the left and right of her body to the side.

It was not a particularly beautiful sight, but when a man squirts, he squirts.

As soon as my orgasm was over, I let myself fall next to her and Isabel immediately wrapped her sperm-smeared body back into the bath-towel and cuddled up to me. She gave me time to catch my breath and then she asked me:

"Was it as good for you as it was for me?"

In my mind, I answered, no, it was better for me, because my orgasm was real, yours was fake, but loudly I said:

"It was wonderful! And now I need the cigarette after sex. "

Cigarettes after Sex

Isabel asked me, "Will you bring me my cigarettes? They are in my purse on the table in the living room. There should also be an ashtray.

I went to the table, lit two cigarettes, one for her and one for me, picked up the ashtray and went back to her into the bed.

There we lay next to each other. Wordlessly we smoked. I was naked, she was wrapped in the cloth like in a chaste American movie, in which scenes where nipples can be seen are forbidden

"You're damn good in bed," she said after a while.

"You too," I lied.

Then we were silent again.

I lay beside Isabel and smoked and thought: Sex with her was the worst I've ever had.

Maybe I could have lived with her limp, saggy boobs and her wrinkled gestures on her stomach, because otherwise she really was very beautiful.

But her way of always hiding her body, ordering me around, not allowing any other positions, and her thinking that she could fake two orgasms without my noticing, that was totally unacceptable for me.

I decided, instead of agreeing with her again, during the next phone call, I would end the relationship which had just begun.

After we had smoked the cigarettes and the ashtray with the cold cigs was on the bedside table, she suddenly leaned up, looked me in the eye and asked me:

"Was I just a quick fuck close in your pick up game or was it the beginning of a relationship?"

I had not expected such a question. What should I answer to that? Should I confess what I just had thought before? Impossible. No, I could not tell her the truth. So I was silent for a moment, thinking about an answer.

Finally I wanted to tell her: A relationship has to develop, then you will see if it will last forever.

But I had no chance to answer this. It had taken too much time to find this answer.

Suddenly Isabel jumped out of bed and yelled at me loudly:

"Out of my bed, out of my apartment!"

"What's going on, Isabel?" I asked, startled.

"No answer is also an answer. I already understood! Get out of here right now! "

"But Isabel," I stammered, "let's talk."

Instead of saying something, she turned angrily, went into the living room, and finally dropped her bath towel, because now she needed both her hands:

Shocking End

She grabbed my clothes and threw them through the open bedroom door in my direction. My jeans flew on the bed, my shirt, my underpants.

I was still in bed, shocked, staring at her.

"Out, I said! Get dressed and get out!", she yelled. To underline it, she reached for my utensils and started to throw them at me. The lighter flew toward me but slammed behind me against the wall, the packet of cigarettes landed on the bed.

"Get dressed and go! How many times must I say it!", she screamed hysterically.

Now I jumped out of bed and grabbed my clothes which were scattered on the bed. Hastily I put on my underpants and trousers. My purse came flying and hit my head. I picked it up and put it in my pocket. I was dressing my shirt when a pack of chewing gum slammed against my chest.

She did not give me time to button up the shirt.

"Your shoes are here, hurry up, faster, faster!",

Isabel yelled and stepped aside, because now I would come out of the bedroom.

I put on my shoes and wanted to say something, but she was already standing at the front door, opened it and shouted: "Shut up and get out!"

I fled through the door and Isabel slammed it behind me.

Dizzy, I walked down the stairs, out of the tenement, got to my car. Once there, I reached into my pocket, but the car key was not there, where it used to be. I reached into all my other pockets of the jeans but I only found my purse, no keys.

Damn, the key was still in Isabel's apartment.

I went back to the front door. I had to ring the bell and ask about the car key. Crap. Which bell? I did not know her last name. I remembered that she lived on the third floor, the last one of this tenement.

There were two apartments on the third floor. And in front of me there were three rows with two bell buttons in each row.

Isabel's could only be one or the other of the two upper bell buttons. I pressed both bell buttons. No Answer. Neither door-buzzer nor intercom. I rang again. No reaction. I kept ringing

After an eternity of at least three minutes ringing, I finally heard Isabel's angry, loud voice from the intercom:

"What else do you want?", she screamed.

"My car key! It has to be up there! I need my car key! "I shouted back.

"Wait, I'll check it out", Isabel answered.

Finally I heard the sound of the door buzzer, and I could go back inside the tenement.

I was just about to go up the stairs again, when Isabel appeared on the top of the staircase and shouted:

"Do not come up! Here comes your key!"

She threw it down across the stairwell and the keys flew towards me, down all the three floors.

The keys clattered beside me on the floor. I picked them up and looked up at Isabel. She had seen that I had picked the keys.

For her, the case was finally closed.

"Now go away!"

She turned and disappeared.

Sitting in the car, I first buttoned my shirt.

Now I needed a cigarette to calm down.

I wanted to light one and start driving.

But the cigarettes were still upstairs. I remembered that she had dumped me with the cigarettes and the lighter.

I started the car and drove off.

The Kick after the Kick Out

I have never been to this area, I had no idea where I was. I saw a pub.

It was Sunday, afternoon, the sun was shining, there were plenty of parking lots. I parked right in front of the pub and entered it.

It was a dim old-fashioned little pub. Two gentlemen sat at the counter and talked to each other.

I sat down at the other end of the counter and when a waitress appeared in front of me, I said "hello", and I ordered:

"A cold beer and coins for cigarette vending machine, please."

She immediately brought the change, and began to tap the beer. I bought cigarettes from the machine, asked for a light. I inhaled the smoke deep into me. Then the waitress served the cold beer and I emptied half the glass in one go.

With relish, I smoked my cigarette and thought of my expulsion.

My adrenaline dropped back to normal and I enjoyed the feeling. It was wonderful. Details of the experience came to my mind. I had to grin and felt comfortable with it.

It was over. I had been insulted and kicked out. A saying occurred to me: Better an end with horror than a horror without an end.

And I did not have a heartache. On the contrary, I was happy to have had this adventure. I had never experienced something exciting as this adventure with Isabel. Especially this sacking, I had never experienced. And I have never ever experienced anything like that later in my life. I had experienced something unique.

The climax of the emotions was not the orgasm, but the kick which I got from the kick out. With this adventure, Isabel gave me an absolutely unforgettable life event.

Love ends with heartache,

Sex ends with orgasm.

The desire for adventure never ends.

Freedom is Adventure

What Siggi Selector conveys through his stories: The pleasure in being allowed to fly all over the world.

As a single, you can experience more emotionally stirring adventures than in a harmonious partnership. In a committed relationship, it gets boring quickly.

Although sex with a girlfriend is better than with a stranger like Isabel or a whore, good sex does not compensate for the lack of variety and excitement that you never know what happens with the next woman. That's why a steady girlfriend gets boring at some point, no matter how many different positions in different places you may practice with her.

The many divorces are also proof of the fact:

Loyalty ends freedom and adventure,
you experience more adventure being free..

Siggi's life is exciting and driven by testosterone. There are more adventures and books by him.

So far only the following are published in English:

The Beauty was the Beast

This book is also available in German language:

Die Schöne war das Biest

and

Sex and Surprise

Sex and Surprise is a bilingual short story which is told in German and in English. You can read parallel. You can train vocabulary. But be aware:

This is the true story of a one-time sex-adventure with a sex-service-provider. It happened only once and it was unique.

Non-Germans also can learn a bit about brothels in Frankfurt/Main, Germany.

Selector keeps writing and translating,

Please drop me a line, if you want me to publish
more stories like that in English.

Contact, letters to the author:

siggi.selector@online.de

Find Siggi Selector on Facebook and Twitter.

Flying from flower to flower like a bee,
because nature wants all flowers to be sprinkled.